Brady Brady
and the Super Skater

Written by Mary Shaw

Illustrated by Chuck Temple

PUBLISHED BY
BRADY BRADY INC.

Published in Canada in 2005 by

Brady Brady Inc.
P.O. Box 367
Waterloo, Ontario
Canada
N2J 4A4

Library and Archives Canada Cataloguing in Publication

Shaw, Mary, 1965 -
Brady Brady and the Super Skater / written by Mary Shaw; illustrated by Chuck Temple.
For children aged 4-8.

ISBN 1-897169-06-X

I. Temple, Chuck, 1962- II. Title.

PS8587.H3473B7322 2005   jC813'.6   C2005-903884-5

When the newest member of the Icehogs encounters some bad luck,
Brady helps his teammate see that it will take more than "super skating" to improve her game.

Printed and bound in Canada

Keep adding to your Brady Brady book collection. Other titles include:

- **Brady Brady and the Great Rink**
- **Brady Brady and the Runaway Goalie**
- **Brady Brady and the Twirlin' Torpedo**
- **Brady Brady and the Singing Tree**
- **Brady Brady and the Big Mistake**
- **Brady Brady and the Great Exchange**
- **Brady Brady and the Most Important Game**
- **Brady Brady and the MVP**

For Morgan and Daron...and her tape ball

Mary Shaw

For the Brady Brady team,
whose endless dedication makes this dream possible

Chuck Temple

Brady couldn't wait to get to the rink. His coach had promised two things for today's practice – a scrimmage game and a new teammate for the Icehogs.

As Brady walked through the parking lot, he noticed a yellow car. Inside there was a flurry of activity; equipment was flying **everywhere**! Helmet, gloves, pants, pads, pucks, and leotards!

"Leotards??!!" Brady said with surprise.

Suddenly the car door swung open. "Hurry up Caroline, you'll be late for your hockey practice," said a woman, as she accidentally dropped a ballet slipper in the slush.

"I know, I know – and my hair is such a mess!" replied a voice from the back seat.

Brady watched as a girl with a headful of curls jumped out of the car, hockey stick in hand.

He rushed ahead to open the door for her. "Hi, I'm Brady," he said proudly. "My friends call me Brady Brady."

"Thank you Brady Brady," she said, flashing a smile. Brady could feel his cheeks turning red. "I'm Caroline and I'm going to be playing for the Icehogs."

When they arrived at the dressing room, the coach asked Brady to introduce Caroline to the rest of the team.

Brady high-fived his teammates as they arrived, and introduced Caroline as their newest player. Caroline looked around at her teammates and took a seat beside Chester.

As the team got dressed for practice, Caroline brushed her hair anxiously. "I know a helmet is a great thing to wear to keep my brain safe, but it makes a terrible mess of my curls!" she said with a giggle.

"Don't be nervous Caroline," Brady told her. "You'll do fine."
But Caroline didn't feel fine.

On the ice, Caroline took off like a rocket!
The Icehogs could not believe how fast she could skate!

"Hey!" Brady called as he tried to catch up to her.
"Where did you learn to be such a super skater?"
But Caroline didn't answer; she was focused on her skating.

Brady's favorite part of practice was the team scrimmage.
The Icehogs were split into two groups.

Brady raced up the ice with Caroline heading toward the net.
He fed her a perfect pass – but it went right past her stick. When she
finally did get the puck, she fired it at Chester – but it went **waaay**
off to the side of the net. "That's okay," Brady reassured her.
"We'll get it next time."

But the next time,
Caroline missed the net again.

And again.

And again.

Brady had never seen
such horrible luck.

Even Chester felt bad for her
and hoped she would get one past him.

In the dressing room, Caroline didn't seem to mind that she had missed the net so often. She proudly showed her new teammates the biggest ball of hockey tape anyone had ever seen!

When the others took the tape off of their socks, they handed it to Caroline. She smiled as she added it to her tape ball. Caroline knew she was going to love being a member of the Icehogs.

"See everyone at the game tomorrow," she waved as she headed out the door. But when she got into her mother's car, Caroline twirled her hair nervously. She wasn't so sure she was looking forward to tomorrow…

On game day, Brady and Caroline waved at Chester who was munching on popcorn in the concession stand.

"Come on, Chester, game time," Brady called to his friend with a chuckle.

Caroline took a seat in the corner of the dressing room.
Slowly, she took out her skates.

"Hey, Caroline, why don't we toss your tape ball around while we
wait for the others?" Brady suggested, hoping
to make her less nervous.

As Brady helped Caroline pull the huge ball out of the bag, he noticed a clear case with a pair of eyeglasses in it.

"Hey, I didn't know you wore glasses!" Brady said to Caroline.

"Uh…I don't!" she said, snatching the case out of his hand. "They're for…uh…dressing up my tape ball."

Plopping the tape ball on the bench, she placed the glasses on it. "See? Just like a snowman!"

Chester pointed at the tape ball and burst out laughing.
"Hey, it kinda looks like me!" he said.

Caroline quickly put her glasses back in the case and buried them deep in her bag.

Brady could tell she was really embarrassed. He also realized why she always missed the net.

Caroline looked at the ground. "I don't like to wear my glasses. The kids on my other hockey team used to tease me a lot."

Brady shook his head. "Well that's not going to happen on this team. We're the Icehogs, and friends don't tease friends."

Chester nodded in agreement as he pushed his glasses back up his nose.

"You're such a super-fast skater, I bet if you wear your glasses, you'll put that puck in the net today!" Brady told her.

Caroline felt much better. She reached into her hockey bag
and put on her glasses.

When everyone had their uniforms on and skates laced up,
they huddled in the center of the room and began their team cheer.

"We've got the power,
We've got the might,
Caroline wears glasses,
And skates like dynamite!"

It was almost the end of the game, and the Icehogs were winning by one goal. Lining up at the face-off circle, Brady could see that Caroline was flustered. She had really hoped to score a big goal to impress her new teammates.

"I guess these glasses aren't helping me at all," she said.

And then it happened.

A Hound player got the puck and headed straight for Chester.
Caroline, the super skater, took off after him.

The Hound player flipped the puck right between Chester's skates, and the Icehogs watched in horror as it went sliding *slooowly* toward the goal line.

In the instant before the puck crossed the line, Caroline lunged forward and whacked it away with her stick.

The buzzer sounded.

Caroline had saved the game for the Icehogs!

In the dressing room, Caroline whispered to Brady.
"Thank you Brady, for making me see that I needed to *see*!"